ESMERELDA The VERY CURIOUS PEACOCK

Written by Franklin Straus

Illustrated by Bartholomew

CONCORDIA

Publishing House
St. Louis

And God said, "That's good."
Genesis 1

DESTRUCTIVE DAVID

Copyright © 1980 by Concordia Publishing House
3558 South Jefferson Avenue, St. Louis, MO 63118

Printed in the United States of America

Library of Congress Cataloging in Publication Data

Straus, Franklin, 1915—
    Destructive David.

    SUMMARY: David is a very destructive boy until he meets a large, natural sculpture named Esmerelda.
    [1. Conduct of Life—Fiction] I. Bartholomew.
II. Title.
PZ7.S9123De   [E]   79-27663
ISBN 0-570-03483-3

To Roz, who has shared in my work
and belief in Esmerelda, this
is my very special gratitude and
thanks.

INTRODUCTION

Who and what is Esmerelda?

Esmerelda is what artists, like myself, call a "natural sculpture." She was made from nature. Since her natural birth, oh, six, seven months ago, I've been asking myself, *Who is Esmerelda?*

She began as just a half-buried, miserable piece of driftwood lying among the sun-dried leaves in a section of woods. How long had she been there on that hillside overlooking the vast blue ocean? I remember lifting her from the stubborn earth and shouting praise and admiration that somehow didn't match her messy appearance. Just then, from somewhere up on the hill, there came the sound of church bells. It didn't break the spell, but made it a very special moment.

Was she aware of being shaped and groomed? Did she know that she was being prepared to meet challenges of worlds unknown to her? Of course not, I told myself. But I still couldn't help but wonder as I began to attach a fan shaped frame to her body. Each and every variety of bird feathers I picked to be part of her crest and her tail had a purpose—but to top them all off I added three colorful peacock feathers.

I gave her a head of pine cone, a beak of razor shells, and a crest arranged with black and white feathers. Finally, two round snail shells used for eyes gave her a commanding view of all the work yet to come.

My wife Roz looked at my work with warm brown eyes. She is my friend and helper. (I must admit she is a better "feather finder" than I am.)

Finally, the last white feather trim was completed. I stood back with one arm resting affectionately around Roz.

We realized how funny Esmerelda would appear to anyone observing her—all the new and unusual combinations of feathers, and her comical face!

With humor and just a tinge of seriousness, I raised my hand and said, "From this day I name thee Esmerelda, the (Very) Curious Peacock." As I said this a peacock feather brushed my ear. I looked at Roz and whispered a little hoarsely, "Roz, I know it's impossible to believe, but I think I heard her say 'Thanks.'"

Esmerelda was ready to join all the other natural sculptures in an outdoor exhibit that next week in the park. I had no idea how popular she would be. She was an instant hit—especially with children, from tots to teenagers. Maybe it was Esmerelda's appearance that invited fantasy, but do you know I watched children actually *talk* to her. (No, I never heard her talk back to them.) There was Rick, a confused and troubled runaway, who stopped by and *told* Esmerelda his troubles. After his talk he decided to go home. There was the day two boys were fighting and suddenly stopped and approached Esmerelda and *asked her* to help settle the dispute. It never fails that I don't walk away shaking my head in disbelief.

Is there God's hand
in the plumage of a bird
a language in the flutter of it's wings
or a message
in the falling of a feather, that awakens
the souls of human beings.

This is the story of one of those children who stopped by to talk to Esmerelda. This is my fantasy—and just one of the many fascinating stories that surround Esmerelda, the (Very) Curious Peacock! Enjoy!

Franklin Straus
Author

David slammed the screen door and hopped off the back steps right on his mother's freshly planted geraniums.

"What do I care," he scoffed. "Dumb old flowers. What good are they anyway."
David didn't see much good in anything.

A small sparrow sat on a tree branch. "Peep, peep," it chirped.

SWISH, David threw a stone at the tiny bird, but it fluttered away just in time. "Stupid bird," David yelled.

David climbed up in the tree. He saw a robin's nest with three tiny eggs inside. SWAT, he knocked the nest to the ground. Luckily, it landed in a bush unharmed.

"That's all we need—more birds chattering and chirping all day long. Who needs them!"

A small spider was carefully weaving her silvery web. PLOP, David took a stick and tore the web down. The spider sailed high in the air. All the hours and hours of hard work had to be done over again.

'EEky old spiders. I hate them!"
David kicked over flower pots, threw rocks at squirrels and rabbits, broke down young trees, and poured soap in the fishpond to get rid of the frogs.

"They're all dumb, stupid things," he said. "I'd destroy them all if I could."

Most of all David liked stepping on anthills.

It was Saturday and David had decided to go to the park, where he could throw rocks at the birds. There he noticed the sign: ART EXHIBIT. He decided to go in for awhile.

Up and down the aisles he walked, looking first at one picture then another. He looked at the large scenic landscapes. He looked at the watercolor seascapes, the wildlife scenes, and the flowers.

"Weird," David said. "Why would anybody want to
buy this junk?"

That's when David saw her. The sign read "ESMERELDA, THE VERY CURIOUS PEACOCK . . . A Natural Sculpture."

Her brightly colored feathers glistened in the sunlight.
"Esmerelda, you're ugly," laughed David.
"You're looking only with your eyes," someone said.
"Who said that?" David asked, looking around.

See the valleys and the mountains.

See God's wonderful creation.

See the sun, the moon, the stars. The coming and the going of the seasons.

See the animals, both large and small.

See yourself, David."

"I don't get it," the boy said. "I don't get it at all."

"You will," answered Esmerelda. "You will, when you learn to see with your heart."

If it is . . .
As truly we must believe,
We are here for good and purpose
And not just "by your leave".

Then all that I can call "I"
Has much to seek and give
And much to learn and thank
For the way we really live.

And every living thing
That needs care and love,
More and more I understand
It comes from God above.

And David remembered. During the next few weeks David thought about his conversation with the curious bird in the park.

"Baloney," shouted David. "Frogs and ants, birds and flowers don't have a purpose. Why did God make them?"

But David began to watch. The baby birds had hatched and had begun to try to fly. The mother bird took time to teach her small fledglings how to flap their wings, and David remembered how his mother had taught him how to do things on his own. He smiled.

He looked at the geraniums he had crushed. The warm sun and rain had helped them bounce back, and the flowers were growing strong and straight. David smiled.

The spider had weaved her web again, and with the sun shining on it, it was truly beautiful. It was like . . . like the lace in his grandmother's tablecloth . . . the one she used at Thanksgiving.

The ants had rebuilt their home again. David watched as two ants carried a load much, much larger than they were.

They managed it by working together. How simple it was when they did it together.

David stood up. "I'm sorry, God," whispered David. "Everything You created is good and for a purpose. Help me to understand that and to have purpose in my life."

It was Saturday again.

"Esmerelda, Esmerelda!" David shouted. "I know what you were trying to show me now. Before I looked with my eyes instead of my heart."

"Excuse me," said a man standing near. "Are you talking to this dried-up piece of driftwood with feathers stuck in it?"

"Is that all you see?" asked David.

The man didn't answer; he just walked away shaking his head.

David smiled, but if the man had been looking—really looking—he would have seen Esmerelda wink her eye.